stories for Girls

LITTLE TIGER PRESS

London

Contents

A Little Fairy Magic

Julia Hubery * Alison Edgson

Phoebe was fizzing with excitement in her new fairy costume. She loved her shimmery wings and her floaty pink dress.

"Look at my wings! Look at my starry wand!" she squeaked, twirling and whirling.

"Now I'm a real, real fairy!" she sang, as she spun and danced.

"You're a fairy princess," smiled Daddy, "and you need an enchanted castle. Come and look . . ."

Phoebe peeped into her bedroom.

"Wow!" she whispered.
Her bedroom sparkled with stars
and twinkles and silvery sprinkles.
"Make us some magic, Phoebe,"
said her big brother Sam.
"I'm going to fly first!" said Phoebe.

She raced into the garden and scrambled up on to the old tree stump.

"I will fly just like a fairy," she thought.

She stood on tiptoes, and stretched her arms.

She leapt high into the air,
waving her wand . . .

. . . and landed BUMP!
in the flower bed.

"Oh dear," sighed Phoebe, "maybe flying is too hard for a brand new fairy – I'll practise wishes instead."

She decided to start with a wish for Sam.

He was playing pirates in the paddling pool.
"I'm Fairy Fizzwhizz," Phoebe announced.
"Tell me your wish and I'll make it come true!"
"Go away, pesky pixie, or you'll walk the
plank!" Sam growled.

"I'm not a pixie!" Phoebe stamped,
"Now make a wish, or I'll bop you!"
"All right," Sam laughed. "I wish
I had a parrot."

Phoebe skipped happily through the garden.
"What shall I use to magic a parrot?"
she wondered . . .

. . . and there, on a leaf, she spotted a ladybird.

"You'll make a perfect parrot!" she said, and began her spell.

"Ibb-bib-bob –
oh, do stay still!

"Tip-tap-top –
stop flying!

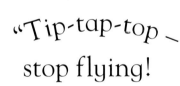

"Oh you mean ladybird,
come back!!!" she shouted,
as it zoomed away.

"I'm not a very good fairy,"
Phoebe sighed to Mummy
and Daddy. "I can't fly,
and I can't magic a parrot."

"Never mind," said Daddy,
"we need some magic – you
can add fairy sprinkles to
the cakes for your birthday
tea – yummy!"

Phoebe made the cakes look so special,
she felt just like a fairy again.
"I'm going to tell Sam I really
can do magic!" she said.

But oh dear, poor Sam
was in a tizz. The mast of
his ship was snapped in two.
"It won't mend," he said sadly,
"now I can't be a pirate any more."

"Don't worry, I'll fix it!" said Phoebe. "My magic's getting better. I just needed practice!"

Phoebe twirled twice, then tapped the mast gently. Nothing happened.

She thought and thought. "I know," she said, "we'll close our eyes, and wish very hard."

Sam closed his eyes, but Phoebe tiptoed to the boat. "One . . . two . . . three . . . fiddle-de-dee . . ." she whispered.

"Ta-daaa!"

Sam opened his eyes . . . and saw a
sparkling new mast on his pirate ship.

"You really can do magic, Fairy
Fizzwhizz!" he laughed.

"I did, I did!" squealed Phoebe,
and they sailed together until
Daddy called, "Ahoy there,
time for tea!"

Mummy and Daddy, Phoebe and Sam shared a fabulous fairy feast.

"I like being a fairy," yawned Phoebe, as the stars began to shine.

"You are a fantastic fairy," said Mummy, "but even fairies need their beds." And she carried Phoebe up to her fairy castle.

As Mummy kissed her goodnight,
Phoebe whispered in her ear:
"I didn't really do fairy magic,
Mummy."

"Oh yes you did," said Mummy.
"You were kind and thoughtful,
and you helped Sam feel
happy – I think that's the best
fairy magic in the world."

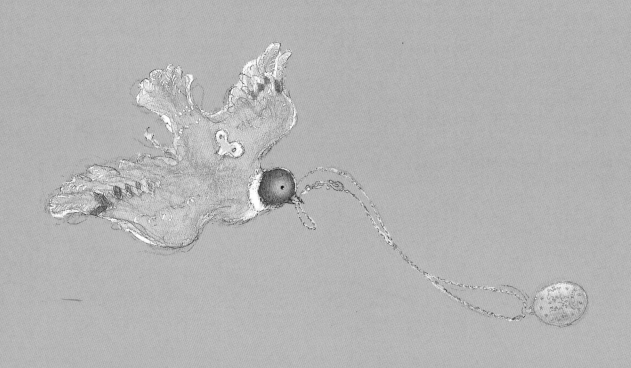

Princess Dolly
and the
SECRET
LOCKET

Alice Wood

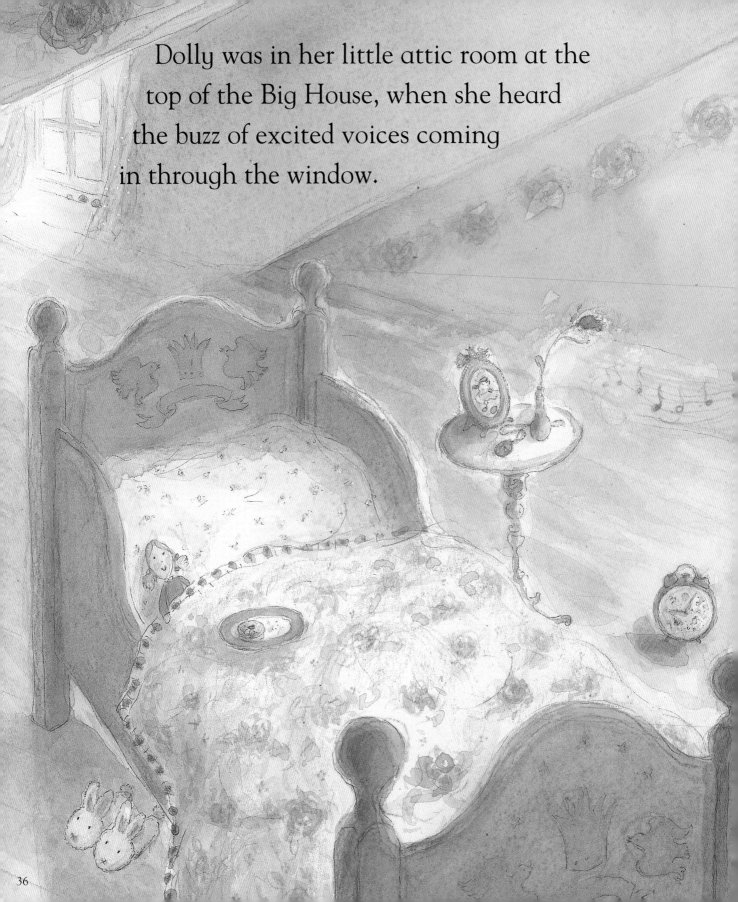

Dolly was in her little attic room at the
top of the Big House, when she heard
the buzz of excited voices coming
in through the window.

"What's going on down there?"
she asked her dear friend Birdie.
"Come on! Let's find out."

Quickly, Dolly tidied away her sewing and put on her special locket, then rushed out along the street.

There was a crowd of people gathered around a big poster. Her friends Sally and Sue were already there, and Cook was reading aloud . . .

The Duke & Duchess
(HOME AT LAST FROM
THEIR WILD TRAVELS)

ANNOUNCE A

Grand Ball
for the
Royal Princess

SATURDAY AT 6 O'CLOCK

THE BALLROOM ~ THE BIG HOUSE

Everyone is invited!

"Well, imagine that!" gasped Cook.
"There's so much to do! Come on, everyone!"
"A real princess, coming here!" said Dolly.
"I wonder what she'll be like."

"Do you think she's very graceful?" asked Sue. "Oh yes!" said Dolly.

"I bet she never gets her hands dirty!" Harry decided.

"She must have lots of servants," said Cook. *That would be nice,* Dolly thought.

"I expect she has baths full of rose-petal perfume and sweet lavender," said Rufus.

"How lovely," Dolly sighed.

Dolly, Sally and Sue scrubbed and polished, dusted and cleaned until the whole house shone. Then they all flopped down at the kitchen table.

"What are you scruffs wearing to the Ball?" asked Cook, eyeing up their grubby clothes. "You want to look your best for the princess, don't you?"

"Ooooh yes!" they agreed.

Dolly fetched her sewing basket and they
chose some pretty material – purple
for Sally and yellow for Sue.

Dolly helped them with the tricky bits and by
suppertime Sally and Sue were clutching
their lovely new dresses and waving goodbye.

But then there was a tap-tap-tapping
on the attic door. Three little toys were
standing outside, looking up at Dolly
with big, round eyes.

"We need your help!" squeaked Teddy.

"Come on in," Dolly smiled.

She stitched a flowery
patch onto Teddy's
trousers . . .

some pink, satin ribbons
onto Lily's ballet slippers . . .

. . . and some pretty flowers
around Bunny's hat.

"You are the kindest Dolly
ever!" they giggled, setting
off home to bed.

Dolly worked late into the evening finishing her own special dress. That night she dreamed of dancing under the shimmering moon while Birdie flew around the bright stars, singing.

Early next morning, there was another knock
at the door. This time it was Sue.

"Oh, Dolly!" she wept. "I tried
on my dress and spilled my juice
and now it's ruined and I've got
nothing else to wear!"

In a heartbeat Dolly decided to give her own special dress to Sue. "Look, I made a spare one, just in case. You can wear it if you like."

Sue blinked away her tears. "You're the best friend *ever!*" she sniffed, and gave Dolly an enormous hug.

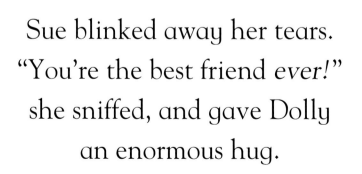

"Oh, Birdie!" Dolly sighed.
"What am I going to wear now?"

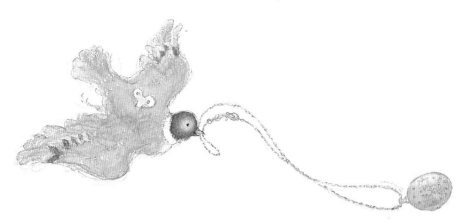

Suddenly, Birdie swooped up into the air.
He dropped something golden and glittering into her lap.

"My locket!" Dolly smiled.
"My dear golden locket! I can
still look my best without
a new dress. I am a
lucky Dolly."

At last it was the evening of the Grand Ball. As the Duke and Duchess stepped out of their splendid coach, everyone gathered round expectantly.

"Greetings to you all on this wonderful evening," said the Duchess. "We are so looking forward to meeting your princess. Is she here?"

Confused whispers rippled through the crowd.

"What does she mean?"

"There isn't a princess here!" Harry called out.
"We thought she was coming with you!"

"Well, this is *very* awkward," said the Duke.
"The princess must be here. She was brought
to the Big House as a baby, years ago.
She would be a little girl by now . . ."

"Really? And we never knew? Whatever could have happened?" asked Cook.

"How will we find her now?"

"She might still have her royal locket," replied the Duchess, "just like mine. Look . . ."

"We know someone with a locket exactly like that one!" called Sally and Sue . . .

"Princess Dolly!"

"Oh my goodness!" Dolly gasped.
"*Me?* A princess?"

"Dear Princess Dolly," the Duchess smiled warmly, "this royal trunk belongs to you." Inside was the most beautiful ballgown Dolly had ever seen.

Sally and Sue helped her try on her precious new things. "We're so glad it's you!" they whispered.

Everybody was delighted. They could
not have wished for a kinder princess
than the lovely Princess Dolly!

The
Tiniest Mermaid

Laura Garnham

Patricia MacCarthy

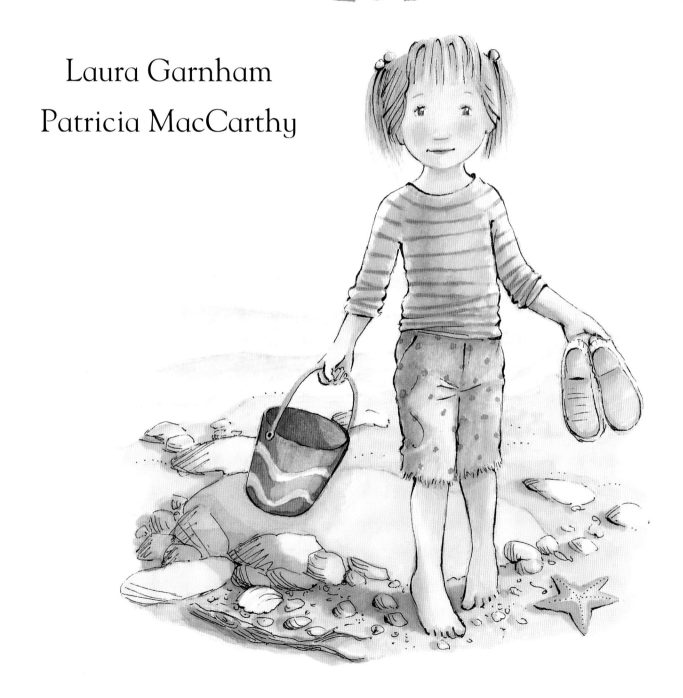

Lily lived by the wide blue sea.
On summer nights she would sit on
the beach, gazing out over the waves,
dreaming of magic and adventure.

One night, as she sat by the rock pools,
a faint sparkle caught her eye and a little
voice cried out, "Help! Please help me!"

Lily gasped. It was a beautiful,
tiny mermaid! Was she dreaming?
But the mermaid called out again,
"Help me, please! My tail
was hurt in the storm
last night and I can't
get back home!"

"Oh, you poor thing!" said Lily.
"I'll help you."
　　"Thank you," whispered the mermaid.
　　"You'll be safe with me," said Lily softly.

Lily scooped the delicate mermaid from the water. She walked carefully up the steps, through the house to her room. By her bed was a huge glass fish tank, the perfect place for a mermaid to rest.

As she slipped into the water the tiny mermaid smiled. "I'm Delphi. What's your name?"

"Lily," said Lily, smiling back at her new friend.

That night Lily sat up for a long time, watching over Delphi as she slept. "I just knew mermaids were real," she whispered to the fish. "Now you let her sleep and get better."

The next morning Lily leapt out of bed and rushed to the fish tank. Had it all been a dream?

"You're still here!" Lily cried with delight.

"Of course," laughed Delphi.

"Where else would I be?"

Delphi was looking much better, and Lily
saw that her tail was twinkling gently.
She thought she had never seen anything
so beautiful in all her life.

Lily and Delphi talked all day. Delphi spoke
of a world where mermaids swam through the
coral, playing with sea horses.

That night Lily's dreams were
filled with magic and mermaids
and a special place far,
far under the sea.

Slowly Delphi grew stronger. As her magic returned her tail sparkled brighter, and she transformed the tank into a shimmering underwater wonderland.

Lily raced home after school each day, and she and Delphi talked and talked until they were the best of friends.

"I wish I were a mermaid," said Lily one night.

"It is wonderful," Delphi said wistfully. "We travel the world using our magic to help trapped or hurt animals. And sometimes we use our sparkling tails to guide sailors home through terrible storms."

"Wow!" said Lily in wonder. "I never knew!"

"It's exciting, but it can be very scary," said Delphi. "When I was hurt in that storm, I was separated from my friends by a huge wave and thrown on to the rocks," she sighed. "They must be wondering what happened to me."

Lily gasped. Delphi's friends would be so worried about her!

"Oh Delphi," she cried. "You must go back to your friends!"

"Yes, I must," said Delphi. "But I shall miss you."

"If only we didn't have to say goodbye!" sighed Lily. "I wish I could come with you. Or just visit your magical world."

Delphi smiled suddenly. "I could show you, if you like. Close your eyes . . ."

Lily took a deep breath as Delphi started singing a gentle, lilting song. Lily could feel magic all round her and hear the rush of the ocean growing louder . . .

All at once she was there with Delphi, swimming with dolphins as they danced and dived through the water. Further and further they swam through the warm blue ocean until the setting sun turned the white beaches gold.

When Lily fell asleep that night she could still hear the dolphin's song and feel the sand between her toes.

The next morning Lily cradled Delphi in her hands for the very last time as she carried her to the seashore.

"Don't be sad, Lily," said Delphi softly, and she gave her a special shell. "Whenever you miss me," she said, "put the shell to your ear and you will hear the magic of the sea whispering inside."

With a flick of her tail, the tiny mermaid
swam off. But as she waved goodbye Lily saw
two more shining tails appear at Delphi's side.
Delphi was with her friends and she was safe.
And Lily knew that whenever she missed her
she could listen to the sounds of the shell, for
Delphi would always be near.

The
Wish
Cat

Ragnhild Scamell
Gaby Hansen

Holly's house had a cat flap. It was
a small door in the big door so a cat
could come and go.

But Holly didn't have a cat.

One night, something magical happened.
Holly saw a falling star.

As the star trailed across the sky, she
made a wish.

"I wish I had a kitten," she whispered.
"A tiny cuddly kitten who could jump in
and out of the cat flap."

CRASH!

Something big landed on the window sill outside. It wasn't a kitten . . .

It was Tom, the scruffiest, most raggedy cat Holly had ever seen. He sat there in the moonlight, smiling a crooked smile.

"Miao-o-ow!"

"I'm Tom, your wish cat," he seemed to say.

"It's a mistake," cried Holly.
"I wished for a kitten."
    Tom didn't think Holly
had made a mistake.

He rubbed his torn ear
against the window and
howled so loudly it made
him cough and splutter.

"Miao-o-ow, o-o-w, o-o-w!"

Holly hid under her
duvet, hoping that
he'd go away.

The next morning, Tom was still there, waiting for her outside the cat flap. He wanted to come in, and he had brought her a present of a smelly old piece of fish.

"Yuk!" said Holly. She picked it up and dropped it in the dustbin. Tom looked puzzled. "Bad cat," she said, shooing him away.

"Go on, go home!" said Holly, walking across to her swing.

But Tom was there
before her. He
sharpened his
claws on the swing . . .

and washed his coat
noisily, pulling out
bits of fur and spitting
them everywhere.

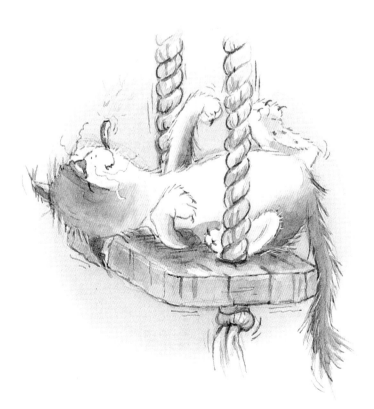

At lunchtime, Tom sat on the
window sill, watching Holly eat.

She broke off a piece of her sandwich and
passed it out to him through the cat flap.
Tom wolfed it down, purring all the while.

In the afternoon, a cold wind swept through the garden, and Holly had to wear her jacket and scarf. Tom didn't seem to feel the cold. He followed her around . . .

chasing leaves . . .

balancing along the
top of the fence . . .

showing off.

Soon it was time for Holly to
go indoors to tea.

"Bye then, Tom," she said,
and stroked his tatty head.

Tom followed her across to the door
and settled himself by the cat flap.

That evening, it snowed.
Gleaming pompoms of
snow danced in the air.

Outside the cat flap,
Tom curled himself into
a ragged ball to keep
warm. Soon there was
a white cushion of snow
all over the doorstep,
and on Tom.

Holly heard him miaowing
miserably. She ran to the
cat flap and held it open . . .

Tom came in, shaking snow all
over the kitchen floor.

"Poor old Tom," said Holly.

He ate a large plate of food, and drank
an even larger bowl of warm milk.

Tom purred louder than ever when
Holly dried him with the kitchen towel.

Soon Tom had settled down, snug on Holly's bed. Holly stroked his scruffy fur, and together they watched the glittering stars.

Then, suddenly, another star fell. Holly couldn't think of a single thing to wish for. She had everything she wanted. And so had Tom.

Fairy Friends

Claire Freedman   Gail Yerrill

Amongst the garden flowers,
In the leafy, dappled light,
The tiny friendship fairies live,
Hiding out of sight!

In their shimmery, secret world,
They love to be together.
Their lives are extra magical
As friendship lasts for ever!

Wishing on a dewdrop,
Sparkling in the sun.
Sharing dreams of happiness
And magic fairy fun!

Catch a glimpse of glistening wing?
Feel a tingle on your skin?

Fluttering fairies are close by,
Sprinkling gold dust as they fly,

Making every dream come true,
Wishing happiness for you!

There's a beautiful petal trail
That leads to a magical place,
Where the scent of rosebuds fills the air
In a patchwork of soft pink lace.

Here the fairies rest their wings
As dragonflies hover above,
For good times are even more special
When shared with the friends that they love.

Puff of stardust on their wings,
Now the fairy fun begins!

Jumping over toadstools,
Dancing with the bees,
Playing catch with ladybirds
In grass as tall as trees.

Swinging on a spider's web,
Skipping with a friend,
Finding golden fairy dust
At the rainbow's end!

Everyone's happy, it's party time!
The fairies have so much to do –
Ballgowns to sew, made from petals,
And ivy-leaf bags to make too!

The fairies all help with the baking,
Piping cream on to tiny iced tarts.
There are strawberry buns and fun fairy fizz,
And sandwiches cut into hearts!

As dusk falls, the lanterns are twinkling,
The garden's aglow in the light.
So, to the soft chime of the music,
Off they fly, for a magical night!

Picking flower petals,
Gathering the dew,
Flying with the baby birds,
Painting rainbows too!

Looking out for others,
Helping someone new,
Making friends with everyone,
That's what fairies do!

Sharing a daisy umbrella,
We hop in a tree hole and hide.
Who cares if it's raining and chilly?
Together we feel warm inside.

When the weather's dull and grey,
Or too wet outdoors to play,
Fairy friends have lots of fun
In their fairy style salon.

Sharing secret fashion tips,
While outside the rain drip-drips.
For, like rainbows after rain,
Friends make you feel bright again!

Best friends know this to be true:
Everything's more fun with two.
Happy chatting, hour by hour,
Curled up cosy, in a flower.

Swapping secrets, holding hands,
Knowing your friend understands,
Sharing wishes from the heart,
Certain that you'll never part.
Talking about anything,
This is what best friendships bring!

At the bottom of the tree stump,
Where the garden almost ends,
There's a spot where all the fairies
Leave out treasures for their friends.

Fairy gifts are made with care,
Like silver snowflake bangles,
Wrapped in petals, moss or leaves
And sparkling moonshine spangles.

Each tiny token means a lot,
A small keepsake to treasure.
For like their special fairy gifts,
True friendship lasts for ever.

When stars glitter in the sky
And the moon gleams up on high,
Under shady ferns we lie,
While the breeze blows like a sigh.
Much too sleepy now to play,
Sharing stories ends our day.

Stars light the sky,
Fireflies flash by,
The garden glows silver and bright.
Shadows soon creep,
Time now to sleep,
Sweet dreams, gentle fairies,
goodnight!

Meet the Fairy Friends!

Being a friend to everyone,
Making your dreams come true,
Always there to show they care,
That's what fairy friends do!

DEWDROP

Dewdrop
is bubbly, talkative
and loves to giggle.

POPPY

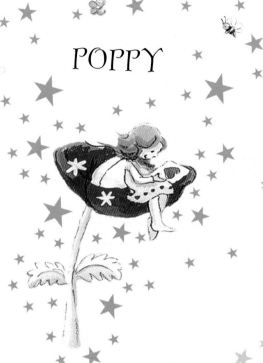

Poppy
is kind, trustworthy
and always sticks up
for her friends.

RAINBOW

Rainbow
is creative, imaginative
and always has
great ideas.

The Princess's Secret Sleepover

Hilary Robinson   Mandy Stanley

I've just been to a sleepover party at my friend Amy's house. Her address is 2 Palace Place. It made me wonder what it's like to sleep in a real palace. I'm going to write to my friend Princess Isabella and ask her.

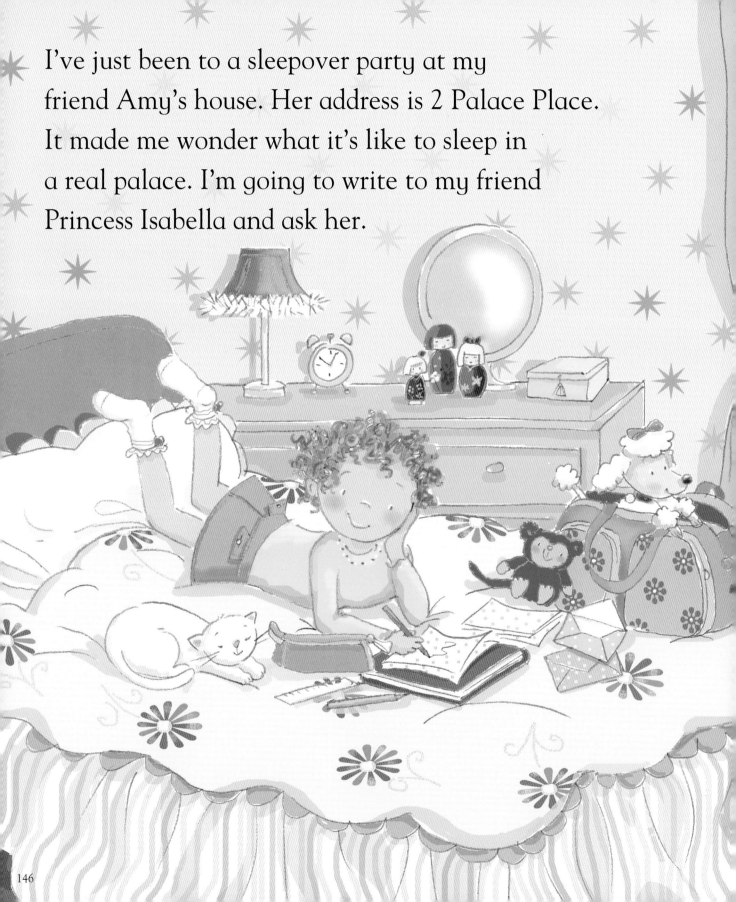

38 Sunny Close,
Townsville

Dear Princess Isabella
I was wondering what it's like sleeping in a palace. Do you have a four-poster bed with curtains on it and are your nighties made from silk?

Love Lucy
x x
x x x

147

Dear Lucy,

Princess Isabella has asked me to write
and thank you for your letter.

The Princess's bed does have satin drapes,
and she has lots of silk nightwear.

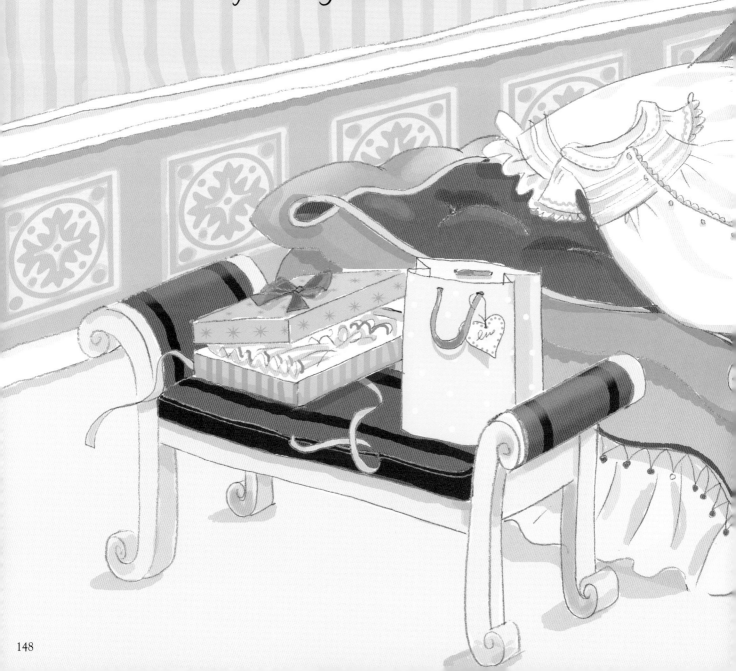

But secretly, she prefers to wear . . .

. . . spotty pyjamas!

38 Sunny Close,
Townsville

Dear Princess Isabella
Thank you for your letter.
My favourite toy dog, Snuggles,
always comes with me to
sleepovers and sits on my
pillow while I sleep. Can you tell
me do princesses have special
toys to watch over them
at night?

Love Lucy

151

Dear Lucy,

  Princess Isabella has asked me to thank you for your letter and to say that she is given lots of beautiful dolls that sit in glass cabinets in her bedroom.

But secretly, her most
loyal guard and friend is . . .

. . . Trusty!

38 Sunny Close,
Townsville

Dear Princess Isabella
Are princesses allowed to
stay up late on sleepovers?
Amy and I make up pop songs
because we want to be famous
one day. We use our hairbrushes
for microphones.

Love Lucy ×
× × ×

Dear Lucy,

Princess Isabella has asked me to write to say that she is allowed to stay up late listening to the royal storyteller.

But secretly, when he's gone
to bed, the royal maids sneak in . . .

. . . to sing in their girl band,
Isabella and the Dusty Daisies!

38 Sunny Close,
Townsville

Dear Princess Isabella
Your girl band sounds great.
Amy and I love making friendship
bracelets and braiding each
other's hair before we go to bed.
Do you ever do that?
× Love Lucy × × × ♡
×
P.S. I'm sending you a ♡
friendship bracelet.

159

Dear Lucy,

Princess Isabella has asked me to write and say thank you for the lovely friendship bracelet. When her cousin Princess Sophia comes to visit, their hair is brushed one hundred times with a silver hairbrush.

But secretly, when no one else
is around, they like to do . . .

. . . face painting!

Last night I had a great idea for something else we could do at a sleepover. I was so excited that I had to write to Princess Isabella to tell her all about it.

38 Sunny Close,
Townsville

Dear Princess Isabella
Next sleepover Amy and I are
going to have Cookies in the
shape of crowns and goblets
of milk. Can you tell me if
princesses are served big banquets
at sleepovers?
+ Love Lucy + ♡ ♡ +

yummy!

milk

Dear Lucy,

The Princess has asked me to write to say that while many royal princesses do eat banquets at sleepovers, the Princess and her loyal friend Trusty prefer midnight feasts. They would be delighted if, on the Princess's birthday this year, you might be kind enough to . . .

. . . join them!

STORIES FOR GIRLS

LITTLE TIGER PRESS
1 The Coda Centre
189 Munster Road, London SW6 6AW
www.littletiger.co.uk

First published in Great Britain 2014

Printed in China
LTP/1800/0981/0914
ISBN 978-1-84895-955-2
2 4 6 8 10 9 7 5 3 1

A LITTLE FAIRY MAGIC

Julia Hubery
Illustrated by Alison Edgson

First published in Great Britain 2011
by Little Tiger Press

Text copyright © Julia Hubery 2011
Illustrations copyright © Alison Edgson 2011

PRINCESS DOLLY AND THE SECRET LOCKET

Alice Wood

First published in Great Britain 2010
by Little Tiger Press

Text and illustrations copyright © Alice Wood 2010

THE TINIEST MERMAID

Laura Garnham
Illustrated by Patricia MacCarthy

First published in Great Britain 2006
by Little Tiger Press

Text copyright © Laura Garnham 2006, 2014
Illustrations copyright © Patricia MacCarthy 2006